Guinea Pigs Don't Talk

By Laurie Myers

Illustrated by Cheryl Taylor

Clarion Books/New York

Clarion Books
a Houghton Mifflin Company imprint
215 Park Avenue South, New York, NY 10003
Text copyright © 1994 by Laurie Myers
Illustrations copyright © 1994 by Cheryl Taylor

The text for this book was set in 13/16-pt. New Baskerville

Printed in the USA

Library of Congress Cataloging-in-Publication Data

Myers, Laurie.
    Guinea pigs don't talk / by Laurie Myers ; illustrated by Cheryl Taylor.
    p. cm.
    Summary: On Lisa's first day at a new school, she and a bossy classmate
begin playing a series of tricks on each other, using the class guinea pigs.
    ISBN 0-395-68967-8
    [1. Schools—Fiction. 2. Guinea pigs—Fiction. 3. Moving, Household—
Fiction.]   I. Taylor, Cheryl, ill. II. Title.
PZ7.M9873Gu   1994
[Fic]—dc20   93-39642
                                                                         CIP
                                                                          AC

VB   10   9   8   7   6   5   4   3   2   1

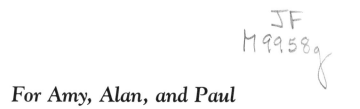

For Amy, Alan, and Paul

Contents

1

Cruisin' for a Bruisin'

"Let me guess," Lisa said, eyeing the two guinea pigs. "This must be Bruiser."

She reached in and scratched the bigger guinea pig. He pushed his head into her hand.

"Right," said Mrs. Flowers.

"And that makes this one Squeaky," Lisa said, reaching into the second cage. When her hand touched the skinny black and white guinea pig, he squeaked and ran in a circle.

"Right again," Mrs. Flowers said. She glided past

the cages, and continued her tour of the class-room. "This is the coatroom." She pointed to a small room directly behind the cages.

Lisa followed Mrs. Flowers.

"And this is your desk," Mrs. Flowers said, gently tapping the top of one desk. "I placed you beside Traci Walters. I think you'll like her."

A possible friend, Lisa thought. Good. First things first. When you get to a new school—make friends.

Mrs. Flowers looked at her watch. "Class starts in about five minutes. You can look around the room until then."

Lisa walked back to the guinea pigs' cages. She had always wanted a guinea pig, but her mother had said, "No pets. It's too much trouble when we move."

"Hello, Bruiser. Hello, Squeaky," Lisa said. "I guess you are my first friends here." Bruiser looked up and purred. Squeaky squeaked.

Friends were exactly what Lisa wanted. Unfortunately, guinea-pig friends were not what she had in mind.

Lisa walked back to her desk and watched the kids come into the room. It was the usual mixture of boys and girls, loud-mouthed and quiet kids, tall and short, curly hair and straight. One girl with dark hair sat in the desk beside her.

"You must be Lisa," she said. "I like your shirt. I have one exactly like it."

Lisa looked down. She was wearing her endangered species t-shirt. It was her favorite.

"You must be Traci."

"How did you know?"

"Mrs. Flowers told me."

"She's a great teacher. You'll love her. She's so . . . flowery." Traci laughed.

Lisa nodded. "She was wearing the biggest earrings I've ever seen."

"The daisies?"

"Yeah."

"Those are big," Traci said. "Mrs. Flowers always wears flowers."

"I'm glad her name isn't Mrs. Onion," Lisa said.

Traci laughed. "Or Mrs. Fish."

They both laughed.

"I'm new too," Traci said. "Well, sort of. I came at the beginning of the year."

"Lucky you," Lisa said. "I hate middle-of-the-year moves."

"Me too. They're the worst," Traci said. "Is your father at the Navy base?"

"No, the university."

"Oh. I didn't think professors moved very much."

"Three times in four years. But he was a student

then; now he's teaching. My mom says we'll be here awhile."

"You got me beat," Traci said. "Two moves in four years. My father's in the Navy. But he says we'll be here at least four years."

"Great!" Lisa said.

Lisa noticed a girl with long white hair walk into the room. A boy with spiked hair was walking with her. They were laughing.

"Who's that?" Lisa asked.

Traci frowned. "Angel and Joe," she said.

Lisa looked at Angel's long, silky hair. It wasn't blond, it was white. She had bright blue eyes.

"She looks like an angel," Lisa said.

"Angel is no angel, and neither is Joe," Traci said firmly. "I've only been here half the year, but I already know about Angel and Joe."

Lisa nodded. "I know the type—always cruisin' for a bruisin'."

"Exactly."

Angel marched down the aisle, and sat two seats in front of Traci. Then she turned quickly and glared at Lisa.

"That used to be my desk until you came," she snorted.

Lisa turned to Traci. "You're right," she whispered. "She's no angel."

Traci smiled.

"Morning glories, it's time to get started," Mrs. Flowers called. Everyone got quiet. "We have a new student. Lisa Rogers."

Lisa tried to smile as everyone stared at her. This was what she hated most about being new.

"We have a busy afternoon planned so we need to take our timed math test this morning before gym," Mrs. Flowers continued. "Everyone get out paper. And I want absolute quiet."

She turned to Lisa. "Since you're new, you won't need to take the test. If you want to, you can feed the guinea pigs, and change the paper in Bruiser's cage."

"Sure," Lisa said.

"Lucky you," Traci said. "I love to take care of the guinea pigs. They're sooooooooooo fun."

Lisa smiled. This was shaping up to be a pretty good first day. She stood to go to the guinea pigs' table.

"Psssssssssst."

The noise came from the front of the room.

"Psssssssssst."

It was Angel. She held a folded piece of paper toward Lisa.

"Me?" Lisa asked, pointing to herself.

Angel nodded.

Lisa wondered why Angel would send her a note. What could Angel possibly have to tell her? Lisa took the note with her to the guinea pigs' table. She had a strange feeling about the note. She remembered Lisa's words, "Angel is no angel, and neither is Joe."

She read the note.

> Put Bruiser in Squeaky's cage
> while you change the paper.
> They love to play.

Is that all? Lisa thought. She felt silly for being suspicious. She refolded the note, and stuck it in her pocket. Maybe Angel wasn't so bad after all. If Bruiser and Squeaky liked to play, then Lisa would put them together. What harm could there be?

2

The Fur Flies

"We must have complete quiet during the test," Mrs. Flowers said. "No distractions. Is everyone ready? Begin!"

The students quickly began working the math problems.

Lisa got the clean newspaper from under the guinea pigs' table. She was especially careful not to crumple the paper or make any noise. She didn't want everyone staring at her again. She quietly lifted the lid off Bruiser's cage.

"You want to play with Squeaky?" she whispered.

Bruiser tilted his head to the side, and looked up at her. He was all brown except for a white streak on his forehead. When she picked him up, he didn't wiggle or squirm. He felt like a solid ball of fur.

When Lisa lifted the lid off Squeaky's cage, he jumped and ran in a circle.

"Company's coming," she cheerfully whispered to him.

"Now keep quiet," she instructed as she lowered Bruiser into Squeaky's cage, "because they're taking a test, and Mrs. Flowers doesn't want any noise."

Bruiser and Squeaky stood face to face. Lisa watched with excitement. She was waiting for them to start a game of guinea-pig tag, romping around the cage, playfully nudging each other with their noses.

No game started.

Squeaky's upper lip quivered, and he scratched the ground with his feet. There were no happy squeaks, as Lisa had expected. Instead, a throaty growl rumbled from the cage.

Squeaky jumped to the side. Bruiser pivoted to face him. Squeaky made another quick jump, then circled around behind Bruiser. Again Bruiser pivoted and they stood face to face—perfectly still.

Lisa had a feeling that this was not the beginning of a friendly game.

Suddenly there was a blur of activity. The guinea pigs had started to fight! Squeaky darted around the cage, jumping at Bruiser and grabbing mouthfuls of his fur. Bruiser bit Squeaky at every opportunity.

They lunged at each other. They rolled around the cage, biting and scratching and knocking over the food bowl.

Lisa was afraid to reach in and stop the fight.

Worst of all was the noise. The guinea pigs squealed loudly, almost screaming, as they fought.

When Lisa looked up, she realized that everyone in the class had turned to watch the commotion.

"Do something," someone yelled.

Lisa turned back to watch the single, rolling ball of fur that was two guinea pigs. She wanted to do something, but her arms hung limply at her side.

Mrs. Flowers jumped up and hurried toward the back of the room.

One girl started to cry. "They're going to kill each other," she said.

Lisa stood by helplessly. Everyone was watching her. She felt her whole face turn red. Mrs. Flowers finally arrived, daisy earrings jingling. As she reached into the cage, Squeaky grabbed Bruiser's ear and bit off a piece.

"*Squeeeeeeeeeeeeeeeek.*" Bruiser's final scream was a loud one. Mrs. Flowers grabbed him and lifted him out of the cage. He was panting.

"You're okay," she said, holding him close to her and stroking his head. She looked at Squeaky. "You're fine too."

"What about the test?" Joe asked.

Mrs. Flowers glanced at her watch and let out a sigh. "We don't have time to finish. I guess we'll have to try it again tomorrow."

The class groaned. Lisa lowered her head.

"I'm sorry, Lisa," Mrs. Flowers said. "I should have told you that Bruiser and Squeaky fight when they are together. That's why we keep them in separate cages."

Mrs. Flowers's kindness didn't make Lisa feel any better. Bruiser was still missing a piece of his ear, even though it wasn't bleeding. It looked like someone had taken a pair of scissors and snipped out a slice.

"Animals can be very territorial," Mrs. Flowers explained.

"What's territorial?" Joe asked.

"When an animal lives in an area, he begins to feel that it belongs to him. He wants to protect the territory, and sometimes he will fight when a new animal comes in, especially if it's another male."

I should have figured that out myself, Lisa thought. Why in the world did I do such a stupid thing? She shoved her hands in her pockets. When she did, she felt Angel's note.

Angel had told her to put the guinea pigs together! That's why she had done it. And Angel had known exactly what would happen.

Lisa's eyes widened with anger. She looked at Angel. Angel was smiling. Her eyes were glued to Lisa. Lisa blinked and turned away. She didn't like looking at Angel. Angel's eyes were . . . She thought for a moment. *Piercing!* That was it. Angel's eyes were piercing.

Piercing eyes looked at you as though they could tell what you were thinking. Lisa didn't like that. Angel Peterson was the last person she wanted to know her thoughts. Because, at that moment, Lisa had only one thought. *Revenge!*

3

The Lunchbox Plan

"That Angel is itchin' for a switchin'," Lisa said. She sat on her bed with her arms folded behind her head.

"Angel is always trying to start trouble," Traci said as she studied Lisa's collection of ceramic animals. She picked up a small tiger. "Angel loves trouble. I think she is addicted to it—like some people are addicted to drugs."

"Do you think she was mad because I had her desk?"

14

"Could be," Traci answered. "Angel's like that. Any excuse to cause trouble."

"That's terrible," Lisa said. "Why does Joe hang around her? She's always telling him what to do. At lunch today she made him get her a straw. Then she made him carry her tray and throw her garbage away."

Traci put the tiger back on the shelf and picked up a monkey. She studied his face. "I guess he's used to it," she said. "He has lots of older brothers and sisters. They're always telling him what to do."

"What about Angel?"

"Nobody tells her what to do."

Lisa fell back on her pillow. "Poor Bruiser," she said. "I feel awful about his ear."

"Don't worry about Bruiser," Traci said, picking up a family of fat pink ceramic pigs. "He's just like these pigs."

"Pigs?"

"Yeah," Traci said. "All Bruiser cares about is eating! That's why he's so fat."

"What does he eat?"

"Anything and everything. Once I made him a shoebox house. He loved to go inside and hide. Then we noticed that the door to his house was getting bigger and bigger. He was eating his house! He loves cardboard."

"Noooooooo!" Lisa said. She rolled across the bed, laughing.

"And at Thanksgiving we had a big turkey made out of construction paper. It was too close to his cage and he ate the head off the turkey."

Lisa grabbed her sides as she laughed again.

"But his very favorite is when kids feed him their leftover lunches. Mrs. Flowers says we shouldn't give him junk because he's fat."

Lisa sat up and wiped her eyes. "Bruiser likes people food?" she said.

"He loves it," Traci said. She put the pigs back on the shelf. "I've even seen him eat broccoli."

"That's it!" Lisa said.

"That's what?" Traci asked.

"That's how I'll get my revenge," Lisa said.

She jumped off the bed and pulled her desk drawer open. She grabbed a pencil and paper.

"What are you doing?" Traci asked.

"I'm going to write a poem," Lisa answered. She tapped the pencil against the paper as she thought.

"For whom?"

"Angel," Lisa said. Then she stopped tapping. "I've got it!" She started to write.

"Angel?" Traci asked. "Why would you write a poem for her?"

"This is not just any poem . . . There!" She firmly dotted the final period on the paper.

"Read it to me," Traci said eagerly.

Lisa cleared her throat.

I think that I shall never see
A guinea pig as hungry as can be.
Bruiser's his name and instead of a fight
He'll eat your lunch when he's out of sight.

"Bruiser is going to eat Angel's lunch?" Traci asked.

"He sure is," Lisa said.

"When?"

"Tomorrow, when I hide him in her lunchbox," Lisa said.

Traci's face lit up. "That's a great idea! Angel has one of those nylon lunchbags with the Velcro top."

"Double perfect," Lisa said. "He'll get plenty of air, and the Velcro will open easily." She paused, then asked, "Do you think that will be too much junk food? I wouldn't want him to get sick."

"Are you kidding?" Traci said. "Angel's mother is a health-food nut. Her lunchbag is probably filled with carrot sticks!"

18

"Perfect for the dieting guinea pig!" Lisa exclaimed.

Traci laughed. "Bruiser," she said, "tomorrow is your lucky day!"

4

Bruiser's Lucky Day

"Turn to page twenty in your science book," Mrs. Flowers said brightly. "This is my favorite unit—flowers!" She began writing on the board. Her necklace of wooden day lilies clinked as she wrote.

Lisa punched Traci and whispered, "The poem is in Angel's science book."

Traci nodded.

The two friends watched with anticipation as Angel opened her book. Her shoulders twitched when she read the note. She turned slowly and looked at the lunch containers, which were lined up by the door. Hers was moving slightly. Angel looked with concern at her lunchbag.

"Angel, what is your favorite?" Mrs. Flowers asked.

Angel quickly turned back to her book. "My favorite? Uh . . . Yummy Tummy Cream Cakes," she blurted out.

Everyone laughed.

"Not food, dear. Flowers," Mrs. Flowers said, fingering her day lilies. "What is your favorite flower?"

Angel looked over her shoulder and saw Lisa grinning. A knowing look crossed Angel's face.

"Venus's-flytrap," she said loudly.

Lisa quickly turned her attention to Mrs. Flowers. She couldn't face Angel. If she did, she would laugh right out loud. She had never been good at hiding her feelings.

"That's not really a flower," Mrs. Flowers said cheerfully. "But it does have a lovely bloom."

Mrs. Flowers went on with class.

Angel spent the rest of science class looking at her lunchbag. When the bell rang, she didn't get up. The other students hurried around the room getting ready to leave.

Joe grabbed his lunchbox. "You coming?" he called to Angel.

"No."

"Okay. I'll save you a seat," he said.

Lisa and Traci stayed in the coatroom as the other children left.

"What do you think Bruiser's doing?" Lisa asked.

"Sleeping," Traci answered. "The lunchbag quit moving about ten minutes ago. How long was he in there?"

"About an hour."

"That means he ate for fifty minutes. Guinea-pig heaven!" Traci said.

Lisa laughed. "I can't wait to see Angel's face when she opens it."

When the last person had left the room, Angel approached her lunchbag. Lisa and Traci peered around the corner.

Slowly, carefully, Angel unhooked the Velcro and opened the bag only a few inches. She peeked inside.

"Oh no," she mumbled.

She gently tilted the lunchbag sideways.

"Where is it?" she muttered.

"What's she looking for?" Lisa whispered to Traci.

Traci lifted her shoulders to say "I don't know."

"Bruiser, I hate to bother you," Angel said. "But I've got to find it."

She opened the lunchbag the rest of the way.

When she did, Bruiser opened his eyes. He stretched his legs and yawned. On his lips was a little dot of white cream.

Angel gasped when she saw it. "That better not be what I think it is," she said.

She lifted him out of the lunchbag.

"Aha! There's the paper," she said. Then she moaned. "It's empty!"

She looked at Bruiser.

"It wasn't your fault," she said, rubbing him between the eyes. "You like them as much as I do."

Angel gently placed Bruiser back in his cage. She walked back to her lunchbag, grabbed it, and dumped the contents into the trash can. Then she stormed out of the room.

"What was she so upset about?" Lisa asked.

"I don't know, but the answer is in that trash can." Traci was already on her way across the room.

When she reached the trash can, she hesitated a moment. She made a face. With the tips of two fingers, she pulled out the shredded wrapper from a Yummy Tummy Cream Cake.

"Angel had a Yummy Tummy Cream Cake!" Lisa said, inspecting the mauled wrapper.

"I can't believe it. Angel Peterson's mother actually bought her a Yummy Tummy Cream Cake," Traci said, shaking her head.

"And Bruiser ate it!" Lisa said. "That's why Angel was so upset."

Traci smiled. "Bruiser does have a sweet tooth."

$$\diamond\diamond\diamond$$

In the cafeteria, Angel stomped over to where Lisa and Traci were eating.

"He ate my Yummy Tummy Cream Cake!" she blurted out.

"Soooooooooo?" Lisa said.

"So," Angel said through gritted teeth. "My mother thinks sugar is the worse thing ever invented. She hardly ever lets me have Yummy Tummy Cream Cakes. I made my bed every day for a week to get that."

Lisa felt bad, but she didn't back down. "Well, my mother thinks sugar is okay," she said. "She lets me have Yummy Tummy Cream Cakes whenever I want."

Angel exploded. "That's it. You have gone too far. Your days are numbered. Boy, am I going to get you. Just you wait."

"Give it a rest," Traci said.

"My Yummy Tummy Cream Cake is gone, and it's all because of her." Angel jabbed a finger at Lisa.

"Hey, you started it," Lisa said. "You're the one who's yearnin' for a burnin'.'"

Angel's face turned red. The truth made her mad. She made her face as mean as possible. Her mouth was a tight thin line. Her eyes were squinted. Her forehead was wrinkled.

"If looks could kill . . ." Lisa said calmly, staring back at Angel.

Angel turned her back on Lisa and stormed to the table where Joe was sitting. She sat down beside him.

"I saved you a place," he said cheerfully.

She ignored him.

"I want revenge," she demanded. "And I want it today."

Joe looked interested. "What kind of revenge?"

Angel smiled. "Guinea-pig revenge."

5

Talking Dogs

After lunch, Mrs. Flowers announced, "Those of you working on the science project come to the science table and finish."

"That's me," Traci said. She left for the front of the room.

"The rest of you read silently," Mrs. Flowers said.

Lisa got out her book and opened to the title page.

"Hey," Joe whispered to Lisa. "Did you know that Squeaky can talk?"

Lisa turned around and looked Joe straight in the eye. "I might be new in this school," she said. "But there are a few things I do know. Guinea pigs do not talk!"

"Squeaky does," Joe said without blinking. He sounded sincere.

"I'll believe it when I hear it," Lisa replied. She turned back in her seat. She didn't want to get into trouble.

"Ask him what his name is," Joe whispered.

So that's the trick, Lisa thought. You ask the guinea pig his name, and he squeaks out two syllables that sound like "Kwwwwwwwwwwwweeeeee keeeeeeee."

Lisa had seen that on TV. People would claim their dog could talk. When they got on TV they would say, "BoBo, what does sandpaper feel like?"

"Ruff, ruff."

"BoBo, what kind of day have you had?"

"Ruff, ruff."

And if BoBo had real talent they would ask, "Are you thirsty?"

BoBo would yawn and growl at the same time. It sounded like "I wan wa wa."

This did not fool Lisa. Squeaky couldn't talk any more than those dogs could.

Lisa glanced to the back of the room. The

guinea pigs' cages stood on a table in front of the coatroom, next to the bookshelf.

Lisa tried to concentrate on her reading, but one thought kept returning—Squeaky. Of course he couldn't actually talk. She was sure of that. But maybe he could squeak his name. It wouldn't be so unusual. After all, dogs got on TV with less talent.

Lisa stood up and walked past Joe to the back of the room.

"Speak clearly so Squeaky can understand you," Joe whispered, snickering.

Lisa ignored Joe. She didn't trust him. He was almost as bad as Angel.

Lisa looked at the books on the bookshelf. Squeaky was on the table to her right. She watched him out of the corner of her eye. He was nibbling on some lettuce.

Lisa looked over her shoulder. Mrs. Flowers was busy grading papers. Now was her chance. She slipped quietly over to Squeaky's cage. She peered in.

"What's your name?" she asked softly.

Squeaky looked up from his lettuce. He stared at her, but said nothing. Maybe he hadn't heard her.

"What's your name?" she asked a little louder.

"Lisa."

She jumped.

"Lisa."

It was Mrs. Flowers.

"We only play with the animals during recess or free time."

"Yes ma'am," Lisa said softly.

Everyone in the class turned around and stared at her. Lisa could feel her neck turn red, then her face. She walked slowly down the aisle, and slumped into her desk. She held her book up in front of her face. She silently vowed not to do anything embarrassing for the rest of her life.

As she gazed at the open book a note fell over her shoulder and landed in her lap. Lisa stared at the note, but she didn't touch it. The note from Angel had caused big trouble. This one might too.

Lisa tried to ignore the note. It was probably from Joe. He did sit behind her.

Lisa knew exactly what she should do. She should pick the note up and throw it right back over her shoulder. She *should* do that—but she didn't.

6

Squeaky Talks

Lisa read the note.

Take this to hear
Squeaky talk.

There was a little arrow pointing to a pink candy taped to the paper. Lisa turned around.

"I know a SweetTart when I see one," she said to Joe. "See, it even has an S on it." She pointed to the S.

Joe leaned forward. He looked Lisa straight in

the eye. "This one is special," he whispered. "Trust me."

"I don't take candy from strangers," Lisa said. "And you are pretty strange." She crumpled the paper into a ball and tossed it on Joe's desk.

Lisa turned away. She tried to concentrate on her book, but she couldn't stop thinking about Squeaky. She was sure he couldn't talk. But it would be fun to hear him squeak his name, like the TV dogs.

Lisa made a decision. She would talk to Squeaky one more time, so she could hear his name. Only this time it would be during recess, when no one was around. That way, there would be no chance for embarrassment.

Lisa waited patiently. When the bell rang, she leaned over to Traci. "You go on ahead and save me a swing. I'll be out in a minute."

When the last person had left the room, Lisa made her way back to the guinea pigs' table. Squeaky was eating. She stooped down so that her face was close to his. He stopped chewing, and stared at her. His small black eyes were not piercing, but friendly.

Lisa looked at him long and hard. There was no doubt about it. He was a regular guinea pig. He said nothing.

Lisa waited.

Still nothing.

She reached in the cage and scratched his head. He purred, but did not talk.

"What's your name?" Lisa asked.

She waited for that familiar high-pitched guinea-pig squeak.

Silence.

Lisa took a deep breath.

"What is your name?" she asked louder.

In a voice as clear as hers he answered, "My name is Squeaky. What's yours?"

7

Achin' for a Breakin'

Lisa jumped away from the cage. She stared at Squeaky. He stared back.

"I said, what's your name?" Squeaky asked. There was no squeak in his voice. He spoke as clearly as any person Lisa had heard.

"Uh . . . uh . . . Lisa," she said.

As soon as she said the words, she regretted answering. She felt silly talking to a guinea pig. She quickly looked over her shoulder to see if anyone had come into the room. She was relieved to find she was still alone.

"This is crazy," she said out loud. "Guinea pigs do not talk."

"I do," Squeaky responded.

Lisa was silent. She looked under the table. No one was hiding underneath. She looked behind her. The room was empty.

"This lettuce they brung me is wilted," he said.

"There's no such word as brung," she said, studying him.

He looked soft and innocent.

"Hey! Will you bring me some new lettuce or not?" He sounded impatient.

Lisa hesitated a moment and then said softly, "Okay."

She turned and hurried to the door. She stopped and looked back. Squeaky was nibbling on his lettuce again. He looked so . . . normal. Lisa shook her head as she left. This was crazy. Guinea pigs did not talk!

When Lisa got to the playground, Joe was standing next to the door, as though he had been waiting for her. She ignored him.

"Want a push?" Traci called from the swings.

"Sure," Lisa said. She climbed onto an empty swing.

Traci pushed and Lisa pumped her legs in and out. She pumped harder and harder. Squeaky was

on her mind. It didn't seem possible that he could talk, and yet she had heard him with her own ears.

She pumped her swing higher.

It wasn't a squeaky sound either. It was a regular voice. It even sounded familiar.

She pumped higher.

She should have looked closer at his lips to see if they were moving.

Higher.

"If you get any higher, you might go over the top," Traci yelled.

Lisa looked down and realized how hard she had been swinging. She extended her legs to slow down. Traci stepped back to watch.

Lisa looked at Traci and decided to ask her about Squeaky. Traci had been in the room all year. She would know if he could talk. Lisa tried to think of the best way to ask the question.

She could say . . .

"Does Squeaky talk?"

No, that was too direct. It should sound more casual. Like . . .

"Just this morning Squeaky said to me . . ."

No, that didn't sound right either. Maybe it should be less personal.

"You know those guinea pigs on the table? Well, I thought I heard one of them say . . ."

No, no, no. Nothing sounded right. Every way she asked the question she sounded dumb. Traci wouldn't want to be friends with someone dumb, and Lisa didn't want to lose the only friend she had.

Lisa swung forward and jumped off her swing. Both feet landed solidly on the ground.

"Perfect landing," Traci said.

"Thanks."

"So, what were you doing in the classroom?" Traci asked.

Lisa studied Traci. After only two days, Traci had become her best friend. It was time for the truth. Lisa took a deep breath.

"Talking to Squeaky," she said.

Traci's eyes narrowed. "Did he talk back?"

Lisa hesitated a moment, then said, "Yes, he did."

"That makes me sooooooooo mad," Traci said.

Lisa looked confused. "Squeaky's talking makes you mad?"

"No," Traci said. "Angel and Joe make me mad. Making Squeaky talk is one of their tricks. Angel stands in the coatroom, behind the guinea pigs' table. She talks for Squeaky."

"That explains it," Lisa said. "I knew that voice sounded familiar. Those two are achin' for a breakin'. And tomorrow's the day!"

Traci's face brightened. "What do you have in mind?"

"Tomorrow we'll carry out my plan for double revenge."

"Double revenge?" Traci said.

Lisa stepped closer. "Angel and Joe get to school pretty early in the morning, don't they?"

"Joe's father brings him on the way to work, so he's the first one here."

"Perfect," Lisa said. "What about Angel?"

"She rides the early bus, so she's usually early too."

"Good," Lisa said. "We'll need to get here before either of them, so we can set up."

"This sounds interesting," Traci said.

"It's more than interesting. It's perfect," Lisa said. "If they think Squeaky talked today, just wait until they hear him tomorrow!"

8

Testing 1, 2, 3

The next morning Lisa and Traci stood in front of the guinea pigs' table.

"Have you got everything?" Traci asked.

"It's all right here," Lisa said, patting her book-bag.

The janitor poked his head into the classroom. "What are you girls doing here so early?"

Lisa and Traci jumped.

"The early bus isn't even here yet," he growled.

Lisa clutched her bookbag and answered truthfully. "We're working on a project."

42

Traci nodded. She held her breath as he studied them. Then he left.

"Whew," Lisa said. "That was close."

Traci nodded. "Let's hurry. We only have a few minutes before Joe gets here."

Lisa was already unzipping her bookbag. She pulled out a ball of wire. A small speaker was attached to one end of the wire. A microphone was attached to the other end.

"When you talk into the microphone," Lisa explained, "your voice travels down the wire, and comes out the speaker."

"I've never seen a speaker that small," Traci said. "Where did you get it?"

"My father's hobby is electronics," Lisa said. "He has lots of stuff like this."

She handed Traci the speaker.

"Tape this behind Squeaky's cage," she instructed. "And be sure to tape it so that no one will see it."

Traci carefully taped the speaker. behind the cage, and then ran the wire down the table leg to the floor. She continued around the edge of the room, unwinding the wire as she went. Lisa followed behind her, taping the wire into place.

When they got to the front of the room Lisa said, "We need to test the speaker."

Lisa switched on the microphone while Traci hurried back to the guinea pigs' table.

"Ready?" Lisa called.

Traci nodded. "Ready!"

Lisa held the microphone close to her mouth. In a high-pitched, squeaky voice she said, "This is Squeaky, the talking guinea pig. Testing one, two, three."

The sound was loud and clear from Squeaky's cage.

"Perfect," Traci giggled. She hurried back to the front of the room.

"Now, where should we hide?" Lisa asked.

They both looked at the only good hiding place—under Mrs. Flowers's desk.

"Do you think we should?" Traci asked.

"It's the only place," Lisa responded. "Besides, Mrs. Flowers will never know. We'll be done by the time she gets here."

Traci hesitated. "Mrs. Flowers is nice, but I don't know how she would feel about us hiding under her desk."

"That's true," Lisa said. "But I'm willing to take a chance."

Traci smiled. "Me too. Hurry. Joe will be here any minute."

They crawled under Mrs. Flowers's desk.

No sooner had they gotten into position than Joe walked in. He was whistling. He headed straight for the coatroom.

"Wait until he comes out," Traci whispered.

Lisa nodded. She held the microphone tightly.

Joe strolled out of the coatroom, past the guinea pigs' table.

"Thanks for the help yesterday," he said with a quick salute toward Squeaky.

Lisa moved the microphone close to her lips. In the high-pitched squeaky voice she answered, "You're welcome."

Joe stopped. He took a small step forward.

"Squeaky?" he said. "Is that you?"

Squeaky tilted his white head up, while Joe stared at the cage.

"That's right, Joe. It's me, Squeaky."

Joe gasped and threw his hand over his heart.

9

The Almost Perfect Plan

"No way!" Joe yelled.

He turned and ran into the coatroom. He looked at the wall where Angel stood when she did Squeaky's voice. No one was there. He raced back into the classroom. It was empty.

He stared at Squeaky.

"I want some Yummy Tummy Cream Cake," Squeaky said.

Joe's mouth fell open.

"Bruiser got some yesterday, and I didn't get any," Squeaky added.

Joe took one step forward. In a soft voice he said, "Squeaky?"

Lisa and Traci could barely keep from laughing out loud.

"What?" Squeaky responded.

"I . . . uh . . . I."

"Spit it out," Squeaky said.

"I can't believe it," Joe said. "You're talking."

Joe felt a tap on his shoulder. He screamed and wheeled around. It was Angel. Joe clutched his chest.

"Don't do that," he said.

"Do what?"

"Sneak up on me."

Angel ignored him. "Do you think Lisa will bring in the lettuce?" She laughed.

Joe's face was serious. "Squeaky doesn't want lettuce. He wants Yummy Tummy Cream Cake."

"What?" Angel glared at Joe.

"Squeaky—wants—Yummy—Tummy—Cream—Cake." Joe said the words as clearly as he could.

"What are you talking about?" Angel asked.

"Squeaky—wants—Yummy—Tummy—"

"I heard what you said," she interrupted. "What I want to know is—are you crazy?"

Joe pulled Angel closer.

"Squeaky really does talk," he confided.

"Yeah right," Angel said.

"It's true!"

"Joe, are you starting to believe your own tricks?" Angel shook her head. "Guinea pigs don't talk!"

"I beg your pardon," Squeaky said.

Angel turned slowly to the cage. Her mouth was open. She looked at Squeaky.

"Hello," Squeaky said.

Angel crossed her arms over her chest, and turned back to Joe.

"How are you doing that?" she asked.

"Doing what?" Joe sounded innocent without even trying.

"Making him talk, dummy."

"I'm not making him talk," Joe said.

"Give the guy a break," Squeaky said. "He's innocent until proven guilty."

"Shut up, you," Angel said, pointing her finger at Squeaky. She turned back to Joe. She shook her finger at him.

"How are you doing that?" she demanded.

"I'm not!"

"You're trying to trick me. You know how I hate that," Angel accused. She lowered her voice as a busload of students came into the room.

"No, I promise," he said. "I was in here by myself, and Squeaky started talking to me."

"Someone has to be doing the talking," Angel said.

She turned and ran into the coatroom. No one was there. She raced out and looked under the table.

"I tell you, it has to be Squeaky," Joe said. "There's no one else."

"I want Yummy Tummy Cream Cake!" Squeaky said.

Angel looked at Squeaky. Then at Joe. "Cut it out," she yelled.

"He forgot his scissors," Squeaky responded.

Joe laughed.

Angel stormed off to her desk. "I'm getting to the bottom of this if it's the last thing I do."

More children shuffled into the room and took their seats.

Lisa bit her lip to keep from laughing. She hadn't had this much fun since she moved here. Traci held her hand over her mouth.

"This is the perfect plan," Traci whispered.

"The only thing left to do is get back to our desks without being seen," Lisa said.

"No problem," Traci said. "We can slip around by the shelves. No one will notice."

Before either one of them could move, they heard some dreadful words.

"Good morning, morning glories," Mrs. Flowers bubbled as she entered the room.

10

Trapped Under the Desk

The class became quiet when Mrs. Flowers entered the room. Lisa completely forgot about the microphone in her hand.

She blurted out, "Oh no! It's Mrs. Flowers!"

The words came out loud and clear from Squeaky's cage.

"Was that Squeaky?" somebody asked.

The whole class stared at Squeaky.

"I told you he could talk," Joe said to Angel.

Mrs. Flowers stopped in the middle of her step. A hush fell over the class as she faced the students.

"Hmmmmmmmmm," Mrs. Flowers said. "Squeaky doesn't sound very glad to see me."

Mrs. Flowers scanned the silent room.

Lisa felt cramped under the desk. Her knees ached. Her back ached. She wanted to stretch her legs, but she didn't dare move.

"I see Traci and Lisa are absent today," Mrs. Flowers said.

Lisa looked at Traci. Traci ran her finger across her neck to show their heads being cut off. Lisa nodded. Traci was right. They were doomed. There was no way out.

Click. Click. Click. Mrs. Flowers's high-heeled shoes clicked across the floor.

"Where's she going?" Lisa whispered.

"Sounds like the back of the room," Traci whispered back.

Click. Click. Click. Silence.

"Squeaky, Squeaky, Squeaky," Mrs. Flowers said. "I'm so sorry that you don't like me."

"I do like you," Lisa said without thinking. Her response was again broadcast from Squeaky's cage to the room.

The class roared with laughter. Mrs. Flowers cleared her throat loudly. The room got quiet.

"I'm glad you like me," she said. "Squeaky, I believe there is something behind your cage. Let's have a look."

Rip. Rip.

Traci made a face. "The speaker," she whispered.

Rip rip rip rip rip.

"The wire," Lisa whispered.

Click. Click. *Rip.* Click. Click. *Rip.*

"She's following the wire around the room," Traci whispered.

"And we know where that leads," Lisa added. She held the microphone out toward Traci.

Click. Click. *Rip.* Click. Click. *Rip.*

"Squeaky!" Mrs. Flowers said. "Guinea pigs chirp. Guinea pigs purr. They even squeak. But I have never heard one talk."

Lisa lifted the microphone to her lips, and in her squeaky voice answered, "We only talk when we have something to say."

Click. Click. *Rip.* The clicks were getting louder.

"Squeaky, you never told me you could talk," Mrs. Flowers said.

"You never asked," Lisa said into the microphone.

Click. Click. Silence.

Traci poked Lisa's shoulder and pointed to the floor between them. Lisa looked down and saw the rosebuds on Mrs. Flowers's high-heeled shoes pointing under the front of the desk. Lisa felt tension on the wire.

"Squeaky, save us," she said as the microphone slipped from her hand.

The class laughed.

"Come out, girls," Mrs. Flowers called. She rolled the remaining wire into a ball.

Lisa and Traci crawled out to face the class.

Everyone was laughing—except Mrs. Flowers.

11

The Secret Ingredient

Lisa sat at her desk. Her trick had worked, and she felt good about that. Mrs. Flowers had not punished them. She felt good about that too. But something was bothering Lisa. She had two enemies—Angel and Joe.

Lisa had two enemies, and this was only her third day in her new school. That was almost one enemy per day. If she kept this up, by the end of the week she would have five enemies. And in two weeks—ten enemies. By the end of the year she would be the number-one enemy in the school. That was not what she wanted.

Lisa sighed. She had not planned for her first days at school to be like this. Things had simply gotten out of hand. She tapped her pencil on her desk and thought about how it had happened.

It had all started with the guinea-pig fight. Squeaky was being . . . what was it Mrs. Flowers had said? Territorial, that was it. Squeaky didn't want anyone new in his territory.

Angel was the same way. She didn't want anyone new in her territory. And in the middle of the school year Lisa had dropped in and taken Angel's desk. Just like Bruiser had dropped into Squeaky's cage.

But Angel wasn't the only problem. Lisa felt a sudden stab of guilt as she realized what had made the problem worse—her own desire for revenge.

Revennnnnnnnnge. The word suited its meaning. It sounded good, and it felt good. But there was a problem with revenge. One person's revenge led to another person's revenge. Then double revenge. It kept getting worse. It might never stop, especially with Angel and Joe.

Lisa had to do something, and fast. But what? She needed a solution. She tapped her pencil two more times and the solution came to her. It was risky, and it would require a secret ingredient. But she had no choice. She had to try it.

Lisa looked at the clock. Ten minutes till recess. Perfect. She would try her solution at recess. There were two things she had to do.

First, she pulled out some paper and wrote three notes—all the same.

*Meet me by the slide
at recess.*

Lisa passed the notes to Traci, Angel, and Joe.

Second, Lisa needed to get the secret ingredient. She would have to use her lunch money, which was in her bookbag. She tiptoed quietly to the wall where the bookbags hung. She reached into hers.

"Lisa, what are you doing back there?" Mrs. Flowers's voice startled her.

"Getting something from my bookbag," she answered. Angel, Joe, and Traci were all looking at her.

"Well, I think you've done enough for one day," Mrs. Flowers said. "Plant yourself in your seat until recess."

Lisa quickly grabbed the money and slipped it into her pocket. She hurried back to her desk. When she sat down, she checked her watch

again—five minutes until recess. There was barely enough time to run across the street to Mr. Burber's grocery store to get the secret ingredient.

Lisa slipped out of her desk and made her way to Mrs. Flowers's desk. She knew she was pushing her luck.

"Mrs. Flowers," she said as nicely as she could. "May I please go to the restroom?"

Mrs. Flowers smiled. "Lisa, you're like a busy bee today." She let out a sigh. "Okay, but it's almost recess, so meet us on the playground when you're finished."

"Thanks," Lisa said. She hurried out the door. She had five minutes to make it to the slide.

12

The Truce

Traci was the first one at the slide.

"Where were you?" she asked when Lisa came running up. "What's in the bag? And what's this all about?"

"It's about our problem with Angel and Joe."

"Oh that," Traci said. "I was thinking about it this morning. I wonder what they'll do next."

"That's the problem," Lisa said. "They do something to us, then we do something to them. It never ends."

"And it keeps getting worse," Traci added.

"Well, I have a plan," Lisa said. "And if it works, the problem will be over. Hey. Here they come."

Angel marched up to the slide. She folded her arms over her chest. "Well, what do you want?" she asked.

"Yeah, what do you want?" Joe echoed. He stood beside Angel.

Lisa took a deep breath. It was now or never. "Let's call a truce," she said firmly.

"A truce?" Joe asked. "What's that?"

"It means that we don't trick you anymore, and you don't trick us," Lisa explained. "No more revenge."

Joe stared at Lisa and Traci. He looked at Angel, then back at Lisa. "Yeah, sure," he said. "Like we can trust you."

Angel said nothing.

"I mean it," Lisa said. She knew it was time. She stuck her hand in the bag and carefully pulled out the secret ingredient. She held it out for Joe. He looked at her hand as if she were holding a precious jewel.

"Yummy Tummy Cream Cakes?" he exclaimed.

"It's a peace offering," Lisa said. "There are two in the package. One for you, and one for Angel."

"What'd you do to it?" Joe asked suspiciously.

"Nothing," Lisa said. "Honest. I let Bruiser eat Angel's Yummy Tummy Cream Cake, so I'm replacing it."

Angel still hadn't said a word.

Joe smiled. "Maybe you're not so bad after all."

He took the package, then turned toward Angel. "Angel, it's Yummy Tummy Cream Cakes, your favorite."

"I see what it is," she said. Her eyes were on the creamy cakes.

Joe ripped the package open with his teeth. He pulled out one of the creamy rolls, and bit off the end. Then he held the other roll out for Angel. She didn't move.

Lisa held her breath. Joe had agreed to the plan. But Angel was tougher. Angel's eyes traveled from Joe to Traci to Lisa. They stopped on Lisa. It was those piercing eyes again. Lisa stared back, determined not to back down. The Yummy Tummy Cream Cake stood between them in Joe's hand. This was the moment of truth.

Angel blinked. She took the Yummy Tummy Cream Cake.

"Good," Lisa said. She quickly opened the second package and handed a creamy cake to Traci. "Three cheers for the truce," she said, jabbing her cake into the air. "Hip hip hooray!"

Angel and Traci did the same. Joe held up his half-eaten cake and the four cakes touched.

"Hip hip hooray! Hip hip hooray!" they yelled.

They lowered their cakes and ate them.

"Mmmmmmmm," Angel said with white cream oozing from her lips. "I love these."

Lisa smiled. She was making friends. She glanced at Angel. Well, maybe not *friends*. Angel was more like a non-enemy. But that was okay. It was a start.

Joe shoved the rest of his creamy cake into his mouth and then wiped his hands on his shorts. "Now, how did you get your voice to come out of Squeaky's cage?"

"It's easy." Lisa smiled. "Come over to my house after school and I'll show you." She eyed Angel.

"I'd like to see how it works," Angel said. She added quickly, "Of course I knew all along it was a trick."

"You have to admit, it did sound like Squeaky," Joe said.

The other three looked at him.

"I mean *if* Squeaky could talk he would sound like that."

"But we all know . . ." Lisa began. And the other three joined in, "Guinea pigs don't talk!"

About the Author

Laurie Myers comes from a writing family: both her mother, Betsy Byars, and her sister, Betsy Duffey, write children's books. *Earthquake in the Third Grade*, illustrated by Karen Ritz, was her first book for Clarion. She lives in Augusta, Georgia, with her husband, Michael, and their three children, Amy, Alan, and Paul.

About the Illustrator

Cheryl Taylor makes her Clarion debut with the pictures for *Guinea Pigs Don't Talk*. She lives in New York City.